Bobby Brewster's ~~Pottle~~

Through his appearances on television and
radio, and the story-telling sessions he has held
in libraries, schools and at parties in Australia,
New Zealand and South Africa, as well as in
almost every part of Britain, H. E. Todd can
claim to be the best-known story-teller in the
world.

Here are eight stories about his favourite
character, Bobby Brewster, the boy to whom
the most extraordinary things happen.

Bobby Brewster's Potato

H. E. Todd

illustrated by Lilian Buchanan

KNIGHT BOOKS
Hodder and Stoughton

Text copyright © 1964 H. E. Todd

Illustrations copyright © Hodder and Stoughton Ltd

First published by Brockhampton Press Ltd 1964

Knight Books edition 1979

Second impression 1984

*The characters and situations in this book are
entirely imaginary and bear no relation to any real
person or actual happening*

This book is sold subject to the condition that
it shall not, by way of trade or otherwise, be
lent, re-sold, hired out or otherwise circulated
without the publisher's prior consent in any
form of binding or cover other than that in
which this is published and without a similar
condition including this condition being
imposed on the subsequent purchaser.

Printed and bound in Great Britain for
Hodder and Stoughton Paperbacks, a
division of Hodder and Stoughton Ltd.,
Mill Road, Dunton Green, Sevenoaks,
Kent (Editorial Office: 47 Bedford
Square, London, WC1 3DP) by
Cox & Wyman Ltd., Reading

ISBN 0 340 24715 0

Contents

Introduction

If you have anywhere to try it, why don't you do some gardening? I'm sure your father or mother would be delighted to let you have a piece of ground.

Personally I haven't much time, because since Bobby Brewster started gardening he has kept me busy writing stories about his adventures. You can't be sure, of course, that you will have quite the same exciting adventures in your garden because, you see, although Bobby is quite an ordinary boy, the most extraordinary things always seem to happen to him, don't they?

Anyway, whether you do any gardening yourself or not, I hope you like this ninth Bobby Brewster book.

H. E. TODD

P.S. Thank you, Olive Walker and Anna Herbert, for telling me about your real experiences which inspired me to write Toad in the Hole *and* Busy and Caroline.

Potato Face

Mr Brewster – that's Bobby's father – doesn't like gardening, which is a pity, because the Brewsters have quite a large garden. As a matter of fact he secretly feels rather ashamed of himself about it, and admits that gardening is a hobby that should satisfy any man. It gives plenty of open-air exercise (especially in the digging season) and the fun of watching things grow (that is, if you have planted them in the right place and at the right time). But you can't force yourself to like something, can you, even if you think you ought to like it? And the fact remains that Mr Brewster definitely does not like gardening.

Of course, the place must be kept tidy. Mr Brewster has bought a motor-mower and is very proud of himself for keeping the grass on the lawn short, although actually the mower does all the work and he just walks behind it. He also has a gardener on one afternoon a week – Tuesday.

Not just an ordinary gardener. Oh dear me, no! The gardener's name is Mr Petherick (they call him Pethers for short) and he has green fingers. Do you know what that means? Mr Petherick's fingers aren't actually green in colour – that would look silly – but whatever he sows in the ground grows into a healthy plant, and that is what is meant by having green fingers.

One Tuesday last September Pethers hadn't been working for the Brewsters for more than a month, so the potatoes which he was digging hadn't been planted by him. A funny-looking lot they were, too. All shapes and sizes and full of holes.

'Did you ever see the like of this?' asked Pethers, handing Bobby Brewster a potato. It had a face. It had, really. Quite a distinct face, with eyes, nose and mouth.

'Yes, as a matter of fact I did,' said Bobby. 'But not another potato. It looks just like old Mr Elliott who lives down the road.'

'So it does,' said Pethers. 'I wondered who it reminded me of, and now I know. Can you tell me how it came to grow that shape?'

'I can't imagine,' said Bobby.

'There are lots of stones underground in this potato patch,' explained Pethers, 'and they get in the way of growing potatoes. So the only thing for the potatoes to do is to grow round them. That's how this one grew into such a funny shape.'

'I see,' said Bobby. 'In that case there must be a stone under the ground that looks like Mr Elliott inside out.'

'I never thought of that,' said Pethers, laughing.

'Can I take this to show Mother, please?' asked Bobby.

'Certainly,' said Pethers. 'You can keep it for all I care. It's no use as a potato.'

Bobby ran into the kitchen. 'Who does that

remind you of, Mother?' he asked, putting the potato on the table.

Mrs Brewster looked. She didn't hesitate for a moment.

'Mr Elliott,' she said. 'It's exactly like him. It's even got his moustache.'

And it had. A funny little fuzzy bit in the middle. They both laughed and agreed that they surely must keep it to show Mr Brewster when he came home.

That afternoon, when Bobby was in the kitchen again, he couldn't resist picking up the potato and looking at it.

'It really *is* like a face,' he said to himself.

At least, he thought he said it to himself, but he can't have done, because a voice answered, 'It *is* a face.'

'I beg your pardon?' said Bobby Brewster.

'I said I *am* a face. A potato face.'

'You're a very clever potato face to be talking,' said Bobby. 'And excuse my asking, but are you by any chance a relation of Mr Elliott's? He lives down the road.'

'None whatever,' said Potato Face, and he sounded quite annoyed. 'I never heard of him. In any case, I couldn't possibly be related to a man, could I? As I said, I'm a potato face.'

'I see,' said Bobby. 'I'm sorry I mentioned it. You look so much like him that I thought there *must* be some connexion.'

'Well, there isn't,' said Potato Face, and that closed the subject. But Potato Face had some more to say about something else. 'You can tell your gardener from me,' he said, 'that it's a complete waste of time digging up the potatoes in the patch he's working on at the moment.'

'Why?' asked Bobby Brewster.

'They're a useless crop,' explained Potato Face. 'They're all riddled with wire-worms.'

'Wire-worms?' said Bobby. 'What are they?'

'If you look into my earhole you'll see one,' said Potato Face.

So Bobby looked – and as he did so a little brown squiggly thing, about a quarter of an inch long, crawled out.

'What a horrid-looking thing,' said Bobby. 'It must be very uncomfortable crawling in your ear.'

'It's not as bad as you think,' said Potato Face. '*You* wouldn't like it in *your* ear, but if it wasn't for wire-worms I wouldn't have an earhole at all. Or two eyes and a nose for that matter. My face would be just a blank, and I wouldn't be nearly as good-looking as I am.'

'Like Mr Elliott?' suggested Bobby Brewster.

'I thought we had agreed to leave him out of it,' said Potato Face crossly.

'Sorry, I forgot,' said Bobby Brewster.

'As I was saying,' continued Potato Face, 'you might as well warn your gardener not to dig up the potatoes in that patch. None of them will be fit to eat, I can assure you.'

'What should he do with them? Leave them in the ground?' asked Bobby.

'Not for good,' said Potato Face. 'That would only leave the wire-worms to breed and attack next year's crop again. No, he should leave them where they are for a time, so that more and more wire-worms eat into them. Then, when they are even fuller of wire-worms than they are now, he can dig them up and burn them. They won't be any good to eat, but it will help to clear the ground of wire-worms ready for next year.'

'That's very interesting,' said Bobby. 'Have you any more suggestions?'

'Yes, I have,' said Potato Face. 'When he's finished digging up the potatoes full of wire-worms, he should put some nice manure on the ground. They won't be very pleased I've told you this, but if your ground is made rich with manure, you may not only be free of wire-worms, but eel-worms as well.'

'Eel-worms?' said Bobby. 'Are they like wire-worms?'

'They're worse than that,' said Potato Face. 'They're so small you can't even see them, and they eat up the potato plants before there are any grown potatoes at all, so the whole plant dies away.'

'What horrid things,' said Bobby Brewster.

'Yes, they are,' agreed Potato Face. 'They should definitely be discouraged.'

'I'll see Pethers next Tuesday and ask him to start discouraging them right away,' said Bobby.

So he did.

Pethers was amazed that Bobby knew so much about potatoes. He had already decided himself what to do to prepare the ground for the next year, but he didn't think Bobby would have known all about it.

'What you say is quite right,' he said. 'Who told you?'

Bobby thought it would sound silly if he answered, 'That potato face you gave me,' so he just said, 'Oh, someone or other.'

'He certainly knows his onions,' said Pethers.

'Yes, and his potatoes as well,' said Bobby Brewster.

Well, that's nearly the end of the story. For eating purposes Pethers dug up the potatoes in another part of the garden, and on the patch where Potato Face had been found he just prepared the ground for the next season. And when it came along there was such a beautiful crop of potatoes that the instructions from Potato Face must have been right, mustn't they?

I expect you're wondering what happened to Potato Face, aren't you? Well, I'm afraid he didn't last much longer. The wire-worms ate right through from one ear to the other and met in the middle, so he fell to bits and had to be put in the dustbin. He didn't seem to mind though. After all, as he said, it was far more interesting to have a face and then fall to bits than just to be blank and then be eaten up, however tasty he might have been to the person who ate him. You can't have it both ways, can you?

One last funny thing that happened I really must tell you. Willie Watson came to tea with Bobby, and on the way home from a walk they saw Mr Elliott working in his garden. During tea Willie Watson suddenly said 'I don't want to be rude, but don't you think that gentleman down the road has got a face like a potato?'

And he couldn't understand why all the three Brewsters roared with laughter.

Marigolds with a difference

Before Pethers came to help in the garden, Bobby Brewster thought very little about growing things himself. But both Pethers and Bobby enjoy a chat, and Pethers is so keen on his job that Bobby soon found himself learning quite a lot about flowers. Before long he asked if he could have a little corner of the garden to sow some seeds himself. Pethers said, 'Yes, by all means,' and so it was all arranged.

'What flowers would you like to grow first?' asked Pethers.

'Marigolds,' said Bobby. 'They're my favourites.'

'That's easy,' said Pethers. 'All you need do is to go and buy some marigold seeds and then sow them.'

When Bobby got his pocket-money that day he went to Woolworth's and bought a packet of marigold seeds. He stood near the counter reading the instructions on the back when a very funny thing happened. This is what the instructions said—

'MARIGOLD (*Calendula*) – that's the Latin name for them– Choice Mixed. Sow March – May in ordinary soil on open ground, about nine inches apart and half an inch deep. Position may be shady or sunny, and seeds may also be sown in autumn to flower in spring.

Special note – In dry weather sprinkle the soil with fizzy lemonade.'

Bobby's eyes nearly popped out of his head. He looked again. Yes, it was quite distinct – 'Special note – In dry weather sprinkle the soil with fizzy lemonade.'

Pethers came the following Tuesday and Bobby showed him the packet of marigold seeds. He didn't mention anything but just asked Pethers if he agreed with the instructions on the back.

'Yes,' said Pethers. 'They're very good, especially the special note. In dry weather you have to keep them moist with a little water.'

'With a little *water*, did you say?' asked Bobby in surprise.

'Yes, of course,' said Pethers, 'That's what it says.'

'I see,' said Bobby Brewster. He didn't really, but he went away by himself to think.

'There's only one explanation,' he decided. 'I must have a magic packet of seeds with special instructions that only I can read properly. I'm jolly well going to sprinkle my seeds with fizzy lemonade even if it does seem silly. But I shall have to do it secretly while no one else is looking.'

So he did – and with the most extraordinary results.

Bobby didn't have much difficulty in fizzy

lemonading his seeds. During a very dry spell in May, his mother certainly thought he was spending more money than usual on fizzy lemonade, but that was his affair, wasn't it, as long as he didn't make himself ill. If she had seen him pouring his fizzy lemonade over the flower bed she might have thought he *was* ill, but he took great care always to do that when nobody was looking.

There can't have been anything wrong with the special note, either. Those seeds grew wonderfully well. They sprouted into strong plants and at last the full buds opened into the most magnificent marigolds. A beautiful golden colour they were, like suns shining upwards. Pethers was delighted.

'I've never seen anything like them,' he said. 'You'll have to enter them for the flower show on August bank holiday.'

'Do you really mean that?' asked Bobby Brewster in great excitement.

'Of course I do,' said Pethers. 'And if they don't win first prize for marigolds, I'll eat my hat.'

For a moment Bobby thought it might be worth only winning second prize just to see Pethers eating his hat, but he decided that wasn't very kind – especially as it was a very old straw hat and wouldn't have tasted nice.

He entered his marigolds for the flower show. The night before, just for luck, he secretly fizzy lemonaded them, and on the morning of the show they were carefully picked and tastefully arranged by Mrs Brewster in a glass bowl. Bobby proudly carried them to the show tent with a label attached saying:

'MARIGOLDS (*Calendula*) Choice mixed
Entered by Bobby Brewster'

He could hardly wait for the opening of the show at two-thirty, and he rushed eagerly along the table of exhibits as soon as he was allowed into the tent.

There they were – on a raised part of the table. *His* marigolds, with two gold stars on a card, which said:

'Entered by Bobby Brewster

FIRST PRIZE FOR MARIGOLDS (CALENDULA)
CHOICE MIXED
ALSO SPECIAL PRIZE FOR BEST ENTRY
IN THE SHOW'

Bobby jumped for joy and ran to tell his mother and father the glad news. When they walked back with him a crowd had gathered round the table. A very excited crowd it was, too, and the first thing Bobby heard was a scornful voice that said, 'Fancy giving *them* the first prize for marigolds. They're not gold. They're blue.'

Bobby peeped through the crowd. The voice was right. A very funny thing had happened. His winning marigolds were a brilliant blue.

'What on earth is the matter?' cried Mrs Brewster. 'I *know* they were gold when I put them in the bowl this morning.'

Well – that wasn't all. Someone went to complain to the judges that it wasn't fair to give the first prize for marigolds to blue flowers, but when the judges came over to inspect Bobby's bowl the flowers had turned back into gold again. They had, really! The judges were very annoyed about it, too, and told the person who complained not to waste their time. There was really quite a scene.

But all that was nothing to what happened when Lady Cattermole was giving away the prizes. She stood on the platform surrounded by bowls of winning flowers.

'First prize for the whole show goes to Bobby Brewster,' she said graciously, 'for his beautiful display of mari – hic.'

Everyone laughed. They thought Lady Cattermole had the hiccups, but she hadn't, you know. She never has hiccups in public. It was Bobby Brewster's flowers that had hiccups, through being fizzy lemonaded so often. Lady Cattermole would not be stopped. For the second time she started.

'First prize for the whole show goes to Bobby Brewster, for his beautiful display of mari – '

Then she stopped. She couldn't finish the word 'marigolds' because they weren't gold any longer. They were purple.

Lady Cattermole was equal to the occasion. 'Bobby Brewster has won first prize,' she said. 'For a beautiful display of maripurples.'

Everyone roared with laughter. And not only because Lady Cattermole had used a funny new word. You see, by the time she finished her announcement the flowers weren't even maripurples. They were maripinks!

Well, that settled it. Nobody cared *what* they were called, but they all agreed that Bobby Brewster's flowers certainly deserved the first prize for something or other. What's more, they said nothing like them had ever been seen before and they didn't expect to see anything like them again.

And they haven't.

There's just one more thing to tell you before the end of this story. Whenever Bobby Brewster goes into Woolworth's to buy packets of seeds, he always looks carefully for one with special instructions to 'sprinkle with fizzy lemonade', but from that day to this he has never found one.

So it's no use his fizzy lemonading any other seeds – and I shouldn't try it yourself either, because, take it from me, it won't work unless the instructions say so.

The glove tree

Bobby Brewster started it all by chewing the fingers of his woollen gloves. Have you ever done that? I have. It tastes horrid and leaves nasty little bits of wool in your mouth. Bobby doesn't know why he did it. He wasn't even aware that he *was* doing it until holes began to appear in the ends of the glove fingers. Then one day Mrs Brewster saw him doing it.

'Bobby,' she said, 'take those gloves out of your mouth and hand them to me.'

Bobby did as he was told.

'Really!' said Mrs Brewster, holding them with the tips of her fingers and making a face. 'You ought to know better. They're absolutely disgusting. They're all damp and falling to pieces. You've only had them a few days, but they're ruined already. Gloves don't grow on trees, you know.'

Bobby looked suitably ashamed of himself and the matter was allowed to drop. Then, a day or two later, he came home from school and said, 'Mother, I need a new pair of gloves.'

'Don't say you've been chewing them again?' said Mrs Brewster.

'Oh no,' replied Bobby, quite hurt at the very suggestion. 'This time I've lost one of them.'

'You really are a careless boy,' said his mother. 'When will you learn to be more careful and look after your things? Gloves don't grow on trees, you know.'

Bobby put his remaining chewed glove in the hall table drawer and thought that it would be wise to keep off the subject of gloves for a time.

That evening Mr Brewster came home rather later than usual and Bobby was in the hall to greet him.

'Hullo, Father,' he said. 'Have you had a good day?'

'Quite good,' said Mr Brewster. 'But I've just done a very silly thing. I've left one of my gloves in the train.'

'Oh dear,' said Bobby. 'That *was* careless of you. Gloves don't grow on trees, you know.'

'Who told you that?' asked Mr Brewster.

'Mother did,' said Bobby. 'And when she hears about your lost glove, I expect she'll tell you too.'

And she did.

The next Saturday morning they all went shopping together. When they returned home Mrs Brewster, with a worried look on her face, started feeling in her coat pocket. Then she turned out all the groceries and searched

anxiously amongst the potatoes which were in the bottom of her basket. But she couldn't find what she was looking for.

'Oh dear,' she said, 'I've only got one glove. I must have dropped the other one while I was out shopping.'

'Really!' said Mr Brewster. 'You ought to be more careful.' Then they all looked at each other and said the same words together:

'GLOVES DON'T GROW ON TREES, YOU KNOW.'

And they started laughing.

That afternoon Bobby went to the hall table drawer to find something and the first thing he picked up was his old glove with the chewed fingers. Then a very funny thing happened.

A voice said, 'Your mother's wrong.'

'I beg your pardon?' said Bobby Brewster.

'I said, "Your mother's wrong",' repeated the voice. 'Gloves don't grow on trees indeed! Of course they do.'

'*I've* never seen them,' said Bobby.

'Maybe you haven't,' said the voice. 'But I ought to know more about it than you do.'

'Who are you, anyway?' asked Bobby Brewster.

'I'm your old chewed glove,' said the voice, 'and I'm magic.'

'You jolly well must be,' said Bobby Brewster. 'For one thing you can talk. That's magic enough to start with. And if you can prove to me that gloves *do* grow on trees, you'll be more magic than ever.'

'That's quite simple,' said the chewed glove. 'All you need do is to plant me in your garden. But you must keep it secret and not tell anyone.'

'Plant you in my garden?' said Bobby. 'That seems silly. Besides, what will Mother say?'

'She'll never know,' said the glove. 'I told you to keep it secret and an old chewed glove like me won't be missed.'

'I suppose that's true,' agreed Bobby. 'But what's the use anyway? Who wants a tree to grow a lot of old chewed gloves?'

'There's no need to be rude about me,' said the glove. 'I've already told you I'm magic and that should be enough. Just plant me in your garden as I said and you won't be disappointed. But don't tell anyone.'

'Of course not,' said Bobby Brewster. 'As if I would. I'm sorry. I didn't mean to be rude. I was just surprised at what you said, that's all. I'll do what you suggest and see what happens.'

So he did.

He went straight into his garden and dug a little hole. Then he planted his old chewed glove in it and covered it with earth. And he made quite sure that no one was looking while he was doing it. Not only because he had been told to keep it secret, but also because he still couldn't help thinking that it seemed rather a silly thing to do.

The next Tuesday when Pethers came, he said to Bobby, 'I see you've been planting something in your garden.'

'How did you know?' asked Bobby.

'It's already sprouting,' said Pethers.

'Is it really?' said Bobby in surprise. 'That's jolly quick. I only planted it last Saturday.'

'What is it?' asked Pethers.

'Aha!' said Bobby Brewster. 'That's a secret.'

'I should be interested to know,' said Pethers, 'because it's sprouting in the middle of winter. I've never seen anything quite like it before.'

'No, I don't suppose you have,' said Bobby. 'But I'm sorry. I still can't tell you what it is. As I said before, it's a secret.'

Well, you never saw anything grow as quickly as that plant. In two weeks it was a tree. Not a big tall tree, but a tree all the same, with promising-looking buds. Pethers gazed at it in amazement when he came each Tuesday. He pestered Bobby to tell him what it was, but the secret was well kept.

Then, on the following Saturday morning, Bobby woke up early. It was a jolly good thing he did, too. Although it was only just light, Bobby went out to look at his tree, and what do you think he saw ? The buds had burst into leaf. They had, really. But there was something even funnier than that. Amongst the leaves were three of the most extraordinary things that can ever have grown on a tree. On the top branch was a man's leather glove, on a lower branch a lady's fur glove, and on the bottom branch a pair of boy's knitted woollen gloves. There were, really.

And what is more, the man's and lady's

gloves looked exactly like those that Bobby's mother and father had lost, and the boy's gloves were just the same as Bobby's had been when they were new.

Bobby picked the gloves from the tree and ran into the kitchen where breakfast was just starting.

'Mother!' he cried. 'Look what I've found.'

'Why, Bobby, it's my missing glove,' said Mrs Brewster.

'Try it on and make sure, will you?' asked Bobby anxiously. 'And see if it's the missing hand.'

So she did, and it was.

Then Bobby made his second surprising announcement.

'I've found Father's glove as well,' he said.

'How can you possibly have found my glove?' asked Mr Brewster. 'I left it in the train.'

'Well, here it is, anyway,' said Bobby, handing the leather glove to his father.

'Where on earth was it?' asked Mr Brewster, looking at it, completely bewildered.

'Aha, that's a secret,' said Bobby Brewster. 'Anyway, I found it, didn't I?'

'You certainly did,' agreed Mr Brewster, but he still looked very puzzled.

'And that's not all,' continued Bobby. 'Here are my own gloves again.'

Mrs Brewster looked at the boy's knitted gloves that he was holding.

'They're not your old gloves,' she said. 'Your gloves were all chewed at the fingers.'

'Well, they're *unchewed* again,' said Bobby Brewster. 'You can see for yourself.'

Mrs Brewster did see for herself, and she couldn't understand it at all. She didn't think

it was possible for gloves to be unchewed. But luckily she didn't say anything, and Bobby got on with his breakfast quickly before he had any explaining to do.

Well, that's the end of this extraordinary story. Although it has been difficult, Bobby has still managed to keep his secret. Pethers came again the following Tuesday and scratched his head when he saw that the buds had burst into leaf in the middle of the winter, and he still can't for the life of him think what the tree is. Even with all his gardening knowledge, he could hardly be expected to guess it was a glove tree, could he?

All the Brewsters have been much more careful with their gloves since that day, so Mrs Brewster has never had to say, 'Gloves don't grow on trees, you know.' Which is perhaps just as well, because it would be rude for Bobby Brewster to argue with his mother, and he knows that THEY DO.

Crazy paving

Have you ever tried walking along a pavement without treading on any of the cracks between the paving stones? I expect you have. I often did it when I was a boy, and, between you and me, still do it sometimes if I think no one else is about. It looks so silly when the cracks are different distances apart and you have to take some extra long strides and some tiny little ones.

The other day I was doing it when I found to my horror that a man was standing over the other side of the road staring at me in amazement, so I pretended to be dancing. I soon stopped that, though, when I realized that a grown-up man dancing on the pavement looks even sillier than a grown-up man trying to miss the cracks between the paving stones. The man on the other side of the road evidently thought so too, judging by the expression on his face.

Of course, Bobby Brewster, being an ordinary sort of boy, often goes for silly walks like that. One day he pretends that if he treads on a crack between paving stones by mistake there will be a big bang and he will disappear. The next day, just to make a change, he says to himself that he simply *must* tread on all the cracks, or one of the paving stones will fall down a hole and him with it. He never has, though – disappeared or fallen down a hole, I mean – which is perhaps just as well.

Once a most extraordinary thing *did* happen to Bobby Brewster when he was playing this game, and that is what this story is about. It was during last summer, when Mr Brewster was laying a crazy pavement in the garden. You see Mrs Brewster had grown tired of the old gravel path, because Bobby was always either coming indoors with pieces of grit sticking to his shoes and spreading them all over the sitting-room carpet, or falling over and grazing his knees on the gravel. So Mr Brewster decided to lay a crazy paving, and a load of broken paving stones was delivered to the Brewster house.

Laying a crazy pavement is no easy matter. For one thing the pieces of paving stone are jolly heavy, and you have to do an awful lot of bending down when you sort them out and try to fit the odd shapes together. Poor Mr Brewster was tired out by the time he had finished, and I'm afraid that towards the end he did not take enough trouble to fit the broken paving stones properly, so that some of the cracks between them were wider than they should have been. However, the path looked quite smart, and Mr Brewster was very proud of himself for finishing it at all. Between you and me, he isn't much of a handyman and is inclined to feel proud of himself rather easily when he ever finishes *any* job about the house.

It was on the following Sunday morning that the first funny thing happened. Bobby Brewster went outside and when he saw the odd-shaped paving stones he couldn't resist playing the 'Crack game' on them. This time he decided to *miss* all the cracks and he jumped from one side to the other like a grasshopper. He nearly reached the end of the path, but then he trod PLONK on a wide crack and a most extraordinary thing happened. There was a loud laugh. There was, really. Bobby wasn't laughing at anything himself, and there was no one else about, so he thought he would try it again. PLONK. He jumped on the same crack, and this time there was an even louder laugh, just like a hyena.

'Where on earth is the laughing coming from?' said Bobby Brewster to himself. At least, he thought he said it to himself, but he can't have done, because a voice answered:

'It's coming from here on earth.'

'*Where* on earth,' asked Bobby in surprise.

'Here on earth,' repeated the voice. 'Look down at your feet. It's me. The paving stone you just trod on.'

'What an extraordinary thing,' said Bobby Brewster. 'I've never heard a paving stone laugh before – and, anyway, what have you got to laugh at?'

'Nothing,' said the paving stone.

'That's silly,' said Bobby.

'Of course it's silly,' said the paving stone.

'But if you insist on calling me a crazy paving, what else can you expect? You can hardly expect a crazy paving to be sensible, can you?'

'Perhaps not,' said Bobby. 'I hadn't thought of that.'

'There are lots of things you haven't thought of,' said the paving stone. 'All this ridiculous walking of yours, for instance. One moment you try to tread on all the cracks and put your full weight on my edges – which is jolly painful – and the next moment you deliberately land PLONK on my middle – which is even worse. What's the point of all that jumping about?'

'Nothing,' said Bobby Brewster. 'It's just for fun.'

'Fun indeed,' said the paving stone. 'Now who's being silly?'

Bobby made no reply. There wasn't much he could have said except 'Me', was there?

Then the paving stone spoke more kindly. 'Never mind,' it said. 'Boys will be boys, and now we've cleared that little matter up, I should like to ask you to do something for me.'

'What is it?' asked Bobby.

'For years and years I was an ordinary paving stone on an ordinary pavement,' explained the paving stone, 'until one day someone dropped a heavy packing-case on me and broke me in two. Then, when the pavement was repaired, I was taken away in two pieces and delivered to your house with a lot more like me to fit into a crazy pavement.'

'You were lucky not just to be thrown on a rubbish dump,' said Bobby.

'Maybe,' said the crazy paving stone. 'But the least your father could have done was to take the trouble to lay me properly. The whole point of a crazy paving is to fit the pieces together like a jigsaw puzzle, and yet, when your father got two stones that really were part of the same pavement, he put me down here and my other half right at the top of the path. So here I am stuck next to a complete stranger, and my other half no better off than I am. That's a fine thing, isn't it?'

'I'm very sorry. I'm afraid my father isn't much of a handyman,' said Bobby apologetically.

'Well, now perhaps you'll ask him to re-lay the path, so that my two halves are together again,' suggested the crazy paving stone.

'I'll try,' said Bobby. 'But I can't be sure he'll be willing to do it. He was complaining about his back last night, and this morning he is having great difficulty in bending. I rather think he's had enough of laying crazy pavements for a bit.'

Bobby was quite right. When he pointed out to his father that he had laid two parts of the same stone at opposite ends of the path, Mr Brewster said he didn't think it mattered much and the path looked all right to him as it was. Bobby couldn't very well protest that the crazy paving stone had *asked* to be moved, could he? He thought it would sound silly, and he was quite right.

Not that it made any difference in the end. When the two halves of the crazy paving stone

realized that Mr Brewster wasn't going to fit them together again, they separately formed their own plans. One morning Mr Brewster looked out of the front door and saw to his astonishment that both pieces of stone were lying loose on the lawn and there were two holes in the path where they had been. He was very annoyed and lifted them back into their holes immediately, but it did no good. The next day they were lying out on the lawn again, and after that he firmly cemented them in their places at opposite ends of the path.

Do you think that worked? Not a bit of it. The following morning the two pieces were again on the lawn, and when Bobby Brewster ran out to look more closely he distinctly heard the sound of mocking laughter. After that he managed to persuade his father to lay the two pieces together after all, and move another piece of crazy paving to the top of the path.

And, do you know, from that day to this there have been no more path troubles of any sort, and indeed all visitors to the Brewster house admire the crazy pathway and say how splendidly it's been laid, which makes Mr Brewster very proud of his handiwork.

Naturally, after his extraordinary conversation with the crazy paving stone, Bobby Brewster takes extra care to walk along the path in a sedate way without any of the 'Crack game' nonsense. So, you see, there have never been any more of those curious peals of laughter, which seems a pity in a way, because laughter never did any harm. Especially to a crazy paving stone.

The Brewster martins

Last spring was an exciting time in the Brewster's garden. Of course, every spring is exciting, but last year something very special happened, as you will realize when you read this story.

It started in the usual way, with the daffodils and the cuckoo. When it first arrives the cuckoo is good to listen to, isn't it? After a time it's apt to get monotonous, with the same call on exactly the same notes. 'Cuck-oo, Cuck-oo, Cuck-oo, Cuck-oo' it cries, until you sometimes feel like putting your head out of the window and shouting, 'PLEASE be quiet.' If only it would just sing backwards for once and go: Oo-cuck, Oo-cuck, Oo-cuck, Oo-cuck.' But it never does. At least, I've never heard it. Have you?

Next came the bluebell and blossom time.

Then the swallows arrived, and built a nest by one of the beams inside the Brewsters' garage. This made Pusster, the Brewsters' cat, frightfully excited. He fondly imagined that he stood a chance of catching a swallow and eating it for dinner, and he used to slink about the lawn with a hunting look on his face, and then crouch like a tiger ready to spring. The swallows didn't care. In the end they grew cheeky and dive-bombed him, which hurt his dignity.

Then one day in May some house martins decided to build their nest under the eaves above the Brewsters' bathroom. Smart little birds they were, with slate-coloured backs and white tummies. I wonder why they chose that particular place? Perhaps they liked the sound of

the water clugging away when the bath plug was pulled out.

It was a beautiful nest they made, safe and snug under the eaves. They flew to and fro with twigs and mud and twittered away happily till the fabric was tightly packed and the inside of the nest smooth and soft. Early in June, Mother house martin laid four eggs, and they hatched out into four little cheeping fluffy black pompons, which were never satisfied unless something was being fed into their beaks.

It was at that time that the painters arrived to paint the outside of the Brewsters' house. Poor Bobby Brewster was very worried. What would happen to the baby house martins when their nest was moved? They couldn't stay where

they were, could they, because the stucco was being whitewashed and the guttering painted with smart green paint.

Luckily the foreman was a very nice man called Mr Haddaway and Bobby got to know him quite well through taking him cups of tea.

'Mr Haddaway,' he asked soon after the work started. 'When are you going to paint the bathroom side of the house?'

'Tomorrow,' said Mr Haddaway. 'Why?'

'Because I want you to take great care of the martins' nest above the window,' explained Bobby. 'Some baby birds are nesting there, and if they fall our cat will certainly catch them.'

'I'm afraid I shall have to move it,' said Mr Haddaway. 'I can't just paint round it. Where shall we put it?'

Then Bobby had an idea. 'Do you think we could hang a nest up in its place after you have finished?' he asked. 'I've got a little basket just about the same size as the nest they've built. We could hook it by the handle from the guttering.'

'That's a jolly good idea. We'll try it,' said Mr Haddaway.

So they did.

When Mother and Father house martin were away collecting food, Bobby and Mr Haddaway carefully removed the nest from the side of the house. The baby birds were very frightened, but they were gently moved from the old nest into Bobby's basket. Then, when the painting was finished, the basket was hung on to the guttering with a hook, in the place where the old nest had been.

When the house martin parents returned they looked most puzzled, and twittered questions to each other. 'This isn't the same nest we left,'

they seemed to say. 'But our babies are safe in it and it will do. We can soon make it just as comfy as our old home.'

And they set to work, still singing happily, to add a soft lining of twigs, grass, and mud to the basket.

Of course Bobby was delighted that his idea had worked. He had grown fond of the little birds because they seemed to add such life and gaiety to the Brewster house. And, do you know, the birds seemed to have grown fond of Bobby too. Mother house martin in particular was quite tame, and when Bobby went into the bathroom she peeped round the corner of the window and twittered to him. Bobby was quite certain she was trying to say something, but he never found out what it was.

The growth of the baby house martins was most fascinating to watch. They became fat and feathery, and their cheeping turned to twittering. After a time they started flying. At first they were frightened to go far, and I don't blame them, do you? You'd be too frightened to fly from the bathroom even now, wouldn't you, and you're quite grown up. But, after all, they *were* birds, and later they gained confidence. When they were strong enough, they went for a family fly together. Later in August all the house martins in the district – not only Brewster martins, but Watson martins, and Singleton martins as well – used to meet in the early evening and have a jolly good fly round and round the church steeple before going to bed.

'They're getting ready to fly away for the winter,' said Mrs Brewster to Bobby one evening. 'I'm afraid they'll soon leave us.'

'Where will they go?' asked Bobby rather sadly.

'To South Africa,' said Mrs Brewster. 'They'll all fly away together, thousands of birds thousands of feet in the air for thousands of miles. And when they reach South Africa they'll build their nests on houses just as they do here, and spend the spring and summer there.'

'But spring and summer are over,' said Bobby Brewster.

'Not in South Africa,' said Mrs Brewster. 'Spring's just starting over there. They have their summer at Christmas time, you know. Next March, when their winter's coming, the house martins will fly all the way back here for our spring. With any luck the same birds will certainly build their nest on our house again.'

'The same birds?' cried Bobby. 'Do you mean to say that they can find their way back to this very house after flying for thousands of miles?'

'Yes, I do,' said his mother. 'It's one of the marvels of nature. And, you know, I have a feeling that our house martins will return to this house because they're so grateful to you for giving them a new nest when the old one was moved.'

That night Bobby was lying in bed thinking hard. 'If those birds are as clever as Mother says,' he said to himself, 'they can jolly well find my cousin Martin who lives in South Africa, and spend spring and summer with him. I *do* hope they haven't left yet. I'm sure Mother house martin listens to what I say, and

I'm going to give her Martin Brewster's address. After all, what could be more fitting than the Brewster martins going to live with Martin Brewster?'

The next morning Bobby went anxiously into the bathroom. Yes, the martins were still there. He could hear them twittering together. He sang a little song so that Mother house martin could hear him, and, sure enough, she soon peeped round the bathroom window.

'I have something very important to tell you,' said Bobby, 'so listen carefully.'

Mother house martin turned her head on one side and looked intelligent.

59

'Mother tells me that you're soon going to South Africa. Is that true?' asked Bobby.

The bird didn't actually answer, but she nodded her head, which was just as good.

'I've got a cousin in South Africa,' said Bobby. 'If I give you his name and address, do you think you could find him and build your nest on his house?'

The bird nodded again.

'Good,' said Bobby Brewster. 'Here are the details.

> Master Martin Brewster
> 76 Brettonwood Avenue
> Umbilo
> Durban
> South Africa.

'Can you remember that?'

Another nod, and a very eager one.

'And when you get there,' added Bobby Brewster, 'please give him my love, and tell him I do hope we'll meet one day.'

The bird flew away. Later that morning, just

to make sure, Bobby pinned a piece of paper facing outside the bathroom window, with cousin Martin's name and address on it. And the next morning when the Brewsters got up, they found that the martins had all flown away, and the house seemed quite sad and lonely without them.

This is nearly the end of the story, but not quite. Six weeks later a letter came for Bobby Brewster from his cousin Martin, and this is what it said:

'Dear Bobby,

'We are having a lovely spring here, and it is very exciting because some house martins have built their nest on the side of our house, just over the bathroom window. Very friendly they are, too, especially Mother house martin. She peeps round the window when I'm in the bathroom and twitters at me. I'm sure she's trying to tell me something, but I can't think what it is.'

Well, I can, can't you?

Pigeon in church

On the Sunday morning that the pigeon first flew into church, some of the congregation took very little notice of the service. And I regret to say that the one who looked least at the vicar and most at the pigeon was Bobby Brewster. He wriggled and turned in his seat to follow it when it flew from one window to the other, and for the rest of the time he was catching Billy Singleton's eye and giggling.

Why is it that when something out of the ordinary happens in church it always seems so much funnier than anywhere else? After all, both Bobby Brewster and Billy Singleton had seen plenty of pigeons before without giggling. And, believe me, a fit of giggles in church is a very painful and embarrassing thing to have. Once you start, it is very difficult to stop, and the more you try to hide it, the more it hurts your tummy. I know. I've had several giggling fits in church myself.

Anyway, when the service was over, Bobby Brewster, looking red in the face, walked out of church with his mother and father and they met the vicar at the door.

'Good morning, Bobby,' said the Reverend Roger Urwin (who doesn't miss much). 'That pigeon seemed to be amusing you in church.'

Bobby looked rather ashamed of himself. 'I'm very sorry, Vicar,' he said. 'I'm afraid I got the giggles.'

'So I observed,' said the vicar. 'We shall really have to do something about our pigeons.

It's bad enough when they build their nests in the belfry, but coming to services and distracting all the boys in the congregation is worse still.' Then he turned to Mr Brooker, the verger, who was standing in the porch.

'William,' he said (everyone calls Mr Brooker 'William'), 'how are you going to get that pigeon out of church before evensong?'

'Well,' replied William, 'I shall first open all the windows and then if it doesn't find its way out, I shall put some crumbs on the font and try to catch it that way.'

'I only hope it works,' said the vicar.

That afternoon Bobby Brewster went for a walk by the church, and when he looked in at the open door he saw the pigeon busily pecking crumbs from the font. There was no sign of William, so Bobby tiptoed in to try and pick the pigeon up and carry it outside.

Then a very funny thing happened. The pigeon fluttered to the other side of the font, looked at Bobby, and said: 'Don't be silly.'

'I beg your pardon?' asked Bobby Brewster.

'I said "Don't be silly",' repeated the pigeon. 'Anyone would think I hadn't got the sense to fly out of church by myself when I feel like it.'

'You must have plenty of sense if you can talk,' said Bobby Brewster.

'You'd better tell that to the vicar and the verger,' said the pigeon. 'Opening all the windows and putting crumbs on the font indeed! Not that I object to crumbs. They taste delicious, and you can congratulate Mrs Verger on her cake-making. But I shall leave the church when I feel like it and not before.'

'You couldn't find your way out during the service this morning,' said Bobby Brewster.

'All that fluttering about was an awful nuisance.'

'That's the vicar's fault,' said the pigeon. 'If his sermon had been shorter and more to the point, I might have kept still and taken more notice. Didn't you see how quietly I stood on the window ledge and listened during some parts of the service?'

'I thought you were just tired through all that fluttering about,' said Bobby. 'I didn't realize that you were listening to the service.'

'Well, I was,' said the pigeon. 'It was beautiful, especially the song those boys sang.'

'People don't sing *songs* in church,' said Bobby Brewster contemptuously. 'That was the choirboys singing an anthem.'

'Whatever it was it sounded nice and was jolly interesting too,' said the pigeon. 'It was all about my cousin.'

'Your cousin?' said Bobby in surprise.

'Yes,' said the pigeon. ' "Oh, for the wings, for the wings of a dove." I've got a cousin who's a dove.'

'Have you indeed?' said Bobby Brewster.

'Yes, I have,' said the pigeon. 'If only the vicar would arrange for the service to have more songs and stories about birds, I'd thoroughly enjoy it, and I'm sure that lots of my pigeon friends would come to church as well.'

'I'm not sure the vicar would like that,' said Bobby Brewster.

'He must be a funny sort of vicar if he doesn't like big congregations,' said the pigeon.

'He does,' said Bobby. 'But big congregations of people, not pigeons. Only this morning he was saying that pigeons were making an awful nuisance of themselves, building nests up in the belfry.'

'We must live somewhere,' protested the pigeon. 'Your vicar seems an unreasonable sort of man to me. First he doesn't want us at his services, and then he doesn't even want us in his church at all. I think he's most unkind.'

'He isn't when you get to know him, honestly he isn't,' explained Bobby Brewster. 'He's a very kind man indeed. I'm sure he doesn't realize how you feel about it.'

Then Bobby Brewster had an idea.

'I'll tell you what,' he suggested. 'If I can persuade the vicar to have a special pigeon service, so that you and all your pigeon friends can come, will you promise to persuade them to leave the church belfry and make their nests somewhere else?'

The pigeon looked thoughtful.

'Yes, I think I can promise that,' he agreed. 'The church belfry isn't as comfortable a place as all that, and in any case Grandma Pigeon nearly jumps out of her feathers when the bell-ringers practise on Thursday evenings. But in return the vicar will have to arrange for a very interesting pigeon service.'

'Leave that to me,' said Bobby. 'I'll deal with the vicar. Just come to church with your friends next Sunday and see what happens.'

The next day Bobby met the vicar out for a walk.

'Vicar,' he said, 'I hope you don't think I'm silly, but I want to ask you a favour.'

'Anything reasonable, Bobby,' said the vicar.

'That's the trouble,' said Bobby. 'I'm afraid you won't think that what I ask *is* reasonable. You remember the pigeon that came to church yesterday?'

'Indeed I do,' said the vicar. 'It was a real nuisance.'

'It didn't mean to be a nuisance,' said Bobby. 'Perhaps it did fly about during your sermon, but that was because it couldn't understand.

Didn't you notice how well-behaved it was for the rest of the time, especially when the choir-boys were singing: "Oh, for the wings, for the wings of a dove"?'

'Yes, I suppose that's true,' agreed the vicar. 'But it didn't occur to me at the time.'

'I believe pigeons like church services about birds,' said Bobby, 'and I also think that they might go and live somewhere else if you arrange a special service for them.'

'What makes you think that?'

Bobby couldn't very well say that the pigeon had told him so, could he? The vicar might have thought it was silly. So he said:

'I just think so, sir, that's all. Anyway, there's no harm in trying, is there?'

'That's true enough,' agreed the vicar. 'And it so happens that next Sunday is the day of Saint Francis, patron saint of birds, so it will be an ideal opportunity.'

Well, of course, Bobby Brewster was very anxious to know what was going to happen in church the following Sunday. He didn't tell anyone about his extraordinary conversation with the pigeon, because the more he thought about it, the more he thought he must have dreamt the whole thing.

He hadn't, though. When he walked into church with his mother and father on Sunday morning, they saw a very worried William standing in the porch.

'What on earth will the vicar say?' asked William. 'Just look at that.' And he pointed to the church windows. The ledges on both sides were covered with long rows of pigeons. They were, really. All standing quietly and looking solemnly at the people as they came in.

'Don't worry, William,' said Bobby. 'This week they're all going to behave themselves.'

'I hope so, I'm sure,' said William, but he didn't look convinced.

The Reverend Roger Urwin had prepared the service very carefully. They started with Hymn 240, and there was great interest among the pigeons when everyone came to the bit about 'Happy birds that sing and fly' – but they stood still and didn't fly about themselves, so that was all right. The lesson came from the eighth chapter of Genesis, verses 1–14, and if you will look that up carefully in the early part of your Bible, you'll see why the vicar chose it.

The most surprising thing of all was the sermon. Now pigeons aren't the only ones who might get bored by sermons. Boys – and even grown-ups – are just as bad. But that morning the Reverend Roger Urwin surpassed himself. He told a most interesting story about Saint Francis of Assisi and the birds taken from a book called *The Little Flowers of Saint Francis*. There was no sign of fidgeting from either boys or pigeons. When the sermon was over, everybody sang the hymn 'All things bright and beautiful' with great enthusiasm, and the most enthusiastic cooing came from the pigeons, especially at the words, 'Each little bird that sings.' Then, after the blessing had been pronounced, the pigeons all flew out of the church door in single file, led by Bobby Brewster's pigeon friend who had started the whole thing.

Of course there was great excitement amongst the people who, as usual, gathered outside the porch after the service. All the conversation, instead of being about the Mothers' Union, or the church outing, or the

sale of work, was about the extraordinary behaviour of the pigeons in church.

That's not quite the end of the story. Since that day, to William's great relief, not a single nest has ever been seen in the belfry. And there have been other reasons for the vicar and William both to change their opinion of pigeons. Untidy fallen leaves have been cleared by the pigeons and dropped in the dustbin behind the vestry door. And pigeons attend all weddings in force, not only to coo at the blushing brides, but to clear up all the confetti afterwards. Of course, they prefer the old-fashioned weddings where people throw rice instead. On the morning after, lots of very fat pigeons with tummies full of rice can be seen waddling around the church.

The Reverend Roger Urwin is delighted, and he's making arrangements for another pigeon service when Saint Francis's day comes round again. I have no doubt that there will be a record congregation – of people *and* pigeons.

Toad in the hole

Mr Brewster is a member of the local golf-club. He joined a few years ago when Mrs Brewster told him that his tummy was growing too fat. She said he needed open-air exercise to make him slim again and that an occasional round of golf up on the common might do the trick. It did, too, for a while. But then he started spending too much time in the club-house, so his tummy grew too fat again.

Bobby's mother soon put a stop to that. She joined the golf-club herself, and now they play together and only go into the club-house to change their clothes or get out of the wet. Once a year, too, they dress up for the club dance, which is a very smart affair.

Bobby often goes to the common with his mother and father to watch them play golf. At least, he watches them for a time, but then he

gets bored and wanders away on his own to look for lost golf-balls. One morning he found three and his father gave him five pence each for them. That gave him an idea.

'I have a suggestion to make,' said Bobby to his father later that morning.

'Oh, have you?' said Mr Brewster. 'I've heard some of your suggestions before. What is it this time?'

'I'm going to save up the money I get for finding golf-balls and turn our lawn into a putting-green. You're always getting annoyed when you take too many strokes at golf, and it might help you to improve your putting.'

Mr Brewster was quite touched. 'That's very

thoughtful of you, Bobby,' he said. 'I'll put some money towards it myself.' And Bobby's mother was so pleased with him that she promised to save some of the housekeeping money to swell the fund. With all this saving, it was only a few weeks before they went proudly to the sports shop to buy a putting set.

When you come to think, it seems an extraordinary thing to do to go to a shop to buy some holes, doesn't it? But that is what the Brewsters bought that morning. Of course, they weren't just holes. They were round pieces of metal that were pushed into the lawn after the holes have been dug to stop the sides from falling in. There were some sticks with numbers on the top, too, to stand in the holes when they weren't being used and to show in what direction the game should be played.

As a matter of fact the Brewsters' lawn isn't ideal for a putting-green, because it's rather wobbly. Not that it mattered much. In a way it made the game more interesting, especially for Bobby Brewster when he played against the Brewsters' golfing friends. He knew where all the wobbles were and soon became quite good. Sometimes he even won, much to the delight of most of the grown-ups. I say *most* of the grown-ups, because there was one notable exception. And that was Mr Bompass.

Mr Bompass was not exactly one of the Brewsters' golfing friends, but they sometimes had to play with him when there was no one else about. He was a very important-looking man with a red face who was really a good golfer. But he had one very great drawback. He hated losing. Even in an unimportant game of wobbly putting on the Brewsters' lawn, he couldn't bear to lose. Which was very silly of him, because it made everyone else all the more anxious to beat him. So mark my words – when you grow up, try and be a good loser if you want people to like you.

Now this story started soon after breakfast one Saturday last spring. Bobby went outside to practise putting, and when he hit the ball into the eighth hole there was a loud croak.

'C-R-O-A-K' (or something like that.)

'Goodness gracious, whatever's that?' said Bobby Brewster to himself. At least, he thought he said it to himself, but he can't have done, because as he took his golf-ball out of the hole a croaky voice said, 'It's me, of course.'

'You?' said Bobby in surprise, and when he looked inside the hole he saw a small toad sitting at the bottom.

'Yes, me,' said the toad.

'I've *seen* a toad, but I've never heard one speak before,' said Bobby Brewster.

'I don't suppose you've ever hit a toad on top of the head with a ball before, have you?' said the toad.

'No, I don't think I have,' agreed Bobby.

'But it really serves you right, you know. You shouldn't have been in the hole at all.'

'Why not,' asked the toad. 'Toads often live in holes in people's gardens.'

'Maybe they do,' said Bobby, 'but this happens to be one of our special holes for hitting golf-balls into.'

'It also happens to be a very comfy hole for toads, because the sides can't fall in,' said the toad.

'That's all very well,' said Bobby. Then he suddenly thought how unsympathetic he was being.

'I say,' he said, 'I'm very sorry – I haven't inquired about your head. I *do* hope you haven't got a bruise.'

'No, it doesn't hurt any longer,' said the toad. 'It was only the shock that made me croak. I wasn't expecting a ball to fall on my head.'

That made Bobby think.

'If you *had* been expecting it, what would you have done?' he asked.

'I'd have nodded hard with my head just as

it was falling, to try and push it out of the hole again,' said the toad.

'I see,' said Bobby Brewster, and rather a mischievous look came into his face.

'I want to try something,' he said. 'When I hit the ball towards this hole, I'll cough to warn you it's coming. Then you can nod as hard as you like, and we'll see what happens.'

So that is what Bobby did – and what *did* happen looked jolly funny. The ball ran along the lawn, popped into the hole, and then popped straight out again.

'Just you stay where you are,' said Bobby. 'I'm going to fetch somebody else to play me at putting. When I cough it means that the ball is being hit into this hole. If it's a very soft cough let the ball fall on your head and keep still, but if it's a loud cough, nod as hard as you can, so that the ball bounces out again. Is that quite clear?'

'Perfectly,' said the toad. 'I'm beginning to enjoy this game myself.'

Well, of course Bobby had intended to ask

his father to play against him, but when he went indoors who do you think he found waiting in the sitting-room? Mr Bompass, looking more important than ever.

'Hullo, young fellow-me-lad,' said Mr Bompass (and how Bobby *hates* being called a silly name like young fellow-me-lad). 'I'm waiting to drive your father up to the golf-course. He wants me to beat him at golf again.'

And he laughed so loudly at his own joke that he went quite purple in the face.

'While you're waiting,' suggested Bobby

innocently, 'why don't you play me at putting on our lawn?'

'Very well,' said Mr Bompass. 'I'll show you how it should be done.' And out they went into the garden.

'Not a bad little course,' said Mr Bompass, 'but a bit wobbly. Not nearly as smooth as the one I have at home. What's bogey?'

There was a loud croak from the eighth hole. The toad must have thought Mr Bompass was talking about him.

'My father once went round in twenty-one,' said Bobby proudly.

'That's no good,' said Mr Bompass. 'I'm sure I shall do it in sixteen.'

Well, Mr Bompass started off very well and at one stage Bobby was afraid that he might live up to his boasting. When they had both reached the eighth hole Bobby had taken twenty-two strokes but Mr Bompass only twelve.

'Now,' said Mr Bompass, looking very pleased with himself, 'I shall probably putt this hole in one.'

But he didn't. Bobby coughed loudly, and the ball popped into the hole and out again.

'What a nuisance!' said Mr Bompass.

Bobby didn't bother to cough softly before his own first stroke, because he knew *he* wouldn't do the hole in one. Then Mr Bompass had his second try. A loud cough from Bobby and out popped the ball.

'Tschah!' snapped Mr Bompass.

Bobby's second stroke was a good one, so he coughed softly as the ball ran in the right direction and it fell into the hole and stayed there.

'That makes twenty-four so far,' said Bobby, and Mr Bompass said, 'Well done,' in a very condescending way.

Then Mr Bompass had his third attempt. A loud cough from Bobby – and out popped the ball.

'Confound it,' cried Mr Bompass.

'You'll have to do it this time, or you won't manage the sixteen you were so sure about,' said Bobby.

But Mr Bompass didn't. There was a loud cough and out popped the ball again.

He didn't do it the next stroke either, because exactly the same thing happened.

'I wish you'd stop coughing,' said Mr Bompass crossly. 'You're putting me off my stroke.'

'I'm very sorry,' said Bobby through his nose. 'I've got a horrid cold.' And he sneezed, just to prove it.

Well, after that I'm afraid Bobby went on being naughty. He coughed loudly for each of Mr Bompass's strokes, and the toad must have heard him, because the ball kept popping in and out of the eighth hole. By the time Mr Bompass had taken fifteen strokes Bobby felt he simply had to take pity on his opponent, because Mr Bompass was so purple in the face that he looked as if he was going to burst. Still, fifteen was quite enough. Mr Bompass was so angry that he was careless when he played the ninth and last hole, and so he finished up with a total of thirty-three strokes. And as Bobby took extra care he managed a three and a total of twenty-seven. So Bobby Brewster had won.

At that moment Mr Brewster came out.

'Hullo, Bompass,' he said cheerfully. 'I see you're showing Bobby how to putt.'

And Bobby coughed very loudly, and sneezed as well. Partly to prove what a bad cold he had and partly to hide a laugh.

That isn't quite the end of the story. Mr Bompass was so upset for the rest of the morning that Mr Brewster actually beat him up on the golf-course for the first time. Since that game Mr Bompass has never again asked the Brewsters to play golf with him which, I regret to say, is a great relief to them.

A few days later Bobby went to the sports shop and bought an extra metal hole which he fitted at the bottom of the garden to make a comfortable place for the toad to live without the risk of golf-balls falling on its head. What is more he sometimes takes the toad a special treat for tea. Can you guess what that is? Sardine sandwiches.

Since then they've come to a special arrangement. Whenever Bobby asks the toad to go to the eighth hole, it does so and nods when it hears a loud cough. I'm afraid Bobby won several games against his father that way, before admitting how it was done. Perhaps it was cheating in a way, but Mr Brewster thought it was a grand joke, and now *he* has also made an arrangement with the toad to cough at the eighth hole when he plays certain people. So it can't be a very serious sort of cheating, can it?

At least, I hope not, because they've both won lots of games that way since then, and fully intend to win some more.

Busy and Caroline

Bobby Brewster has a number of grown-up friends, and one of his favourites is an elderly lady who is a neighbour of his called Mrs Anna Herbert. She's a dear old lady and she's very fond of Bobby, because he often calls round to ask her how she is. Whether he'd inquire after her health quite so often if she didn't give him a macaroon every time, I'm not prepared to say. After all, if a dear old lady is 'Very well, thank you,' in the morning, she's likely to be 'Very well, thank you,' in the afternoon as well, isn't she, so the only reason for asking again might well be another macaroon. However, we'll give Bobby Brewster the benefit of the doubt, because he really is kind to Mrs Herbert, macaroons or no macaroons.

Mrs Herbert lives by herself, so it's not surprising that she has a dog. Her dog is a smart little black poodle, and she's a most intelligent and engaging animal. I'm sure she understands every word her mistress says, and she barks furiously whenever anyone approaches the house, so she's very useful as a watchdog. Her name is Busy, and it couldn't be more suitable. Whatever that dog is doing she's busy. Out for a walk, she struts about in a busy way. When she chases a ball – which she does whenever anyone is willing to throw it for her – she catches it on the bounce and busily returns it for another throw. Whilst eating she makes busy chewing noises. She even sleeps with one eye open, which is a very busy way of sleeping. Altogether she's a lovely little dog, and what her mistress would do without her, I'm sure I don't know.

Mrs Herbert has something else of which she's very fond and that's her small garden. Although she's getting on in years, she does all her own gardening, except mow the lawn. She prunes the roses and trims the edges of the

lawn, and forks the flower beds and sometimes –
only sometimes, mind you – Bobby Brewster
helps her with the weeding.

Last spring Bobby decided that he wanted to
give Mrs Herbert a present for her birthday.
She was so fond of her dog and the birds and
flowers in her garden, that he decided something
living would be right for her, as long as it
wasn't too much trouble to look after. At first
he thought of a plant or a rose tree, or something like that, but his mother said that prac-
tically every inch in her garden, except the
lawn, already had a plant in it. Then Mrs
Brewster had a brilliant idea.

'What about a tortoise?' she suggested.

Well, what about a tortoise? Bobby hadn't
thought of that. After all, a tortoise isn't the
sort of thing you *do* think about much, is it?
But the more he *did* think about it, the better
he liked it. A tortoise is easy to feed, and if it
tries to run away, even an old lady ought to be
able to catch it. Above all, it wouldn't be likely
to quarrel with Busy the poodle.

So a tortoise it was. Bobby went to a pet shop and bought one for thirty pence, and on the morning of her birthday he presented it to Mrs Herbert.

She was absolutely delighted, and the first thing she asked Bobby – after she had thanked him, of course – was whether it was a boy or girl. Bobby had forgotten to ask at the pet shop, so he said he was afraid he didn't know.

'Never mind,' said Mrs Herbert. 'I'm going to call her Caroline, anyway, so as far as I am concerned she's a her.'

'Good,' said Bobby. 'That's settled.' Then he remembered the instructions he'd been given by the man in the pet shop.

'She feeds on lettuce and cabbage leaves,' he

said. 'She must be kept warm, and she likes having her chin tickled.'

'Very well,' said Mrs Herbert. 'I'll be sure always to keep a cabbage or a lettuce in the pantry. I'll protect her from the cold, and I'll tickle her chin at least four times a day.'

And from that day to this she always has, except when Caroline has been hibernating – a word which I'll explain later in this story.

I don't know if you've ever had a tortoise of your own. I certainly haven't, and I must admit I've been quite happy without one, because I never thought they were very interesting pets. But Bobby Brewster assures me that I'm quite wrong. He says that Caroline was a delightful creature, very friendly and full of character, and in view of what happened, I'm now quite ready to agree with him. Of course, Caroline didn't skip about and make loud noises like Busy, but she showed her affection in a more sedate way. She waved her head from side to side when she was pleased and nibbled at Mrs Herbert's finger when it was wagged at her.

But her closest friend of all was the poodle.
At first Busy couldn't make Caroline out and
crawled towards her with a puzzled expression.
Caroline kept her head under her shell in case
of trouble. But not for long. When Busy
started licking the shell, Caroline stuck her head
out, and a soppy expression came into her face.
She also waved her neck to and fro. She didn't
actually wag her tail, because her tail isn't the
wagging kind, but she certainly would have
done so if she could. Busy couldn't understand
why Caroline crawled so slowly, and she pushed

her with her paws and nuzzled her with her nose to get a move on. Caroline didn't mind – it was all good fun as long as she was with Busy.

After a time Mrs Herbert thought of a convenient way of picking Caroline up without having to bend too far. She tied two loops of string round her with a string handle at the top for carrying. Of course, the handle was really meant for people, but Busy thought it was a jolly good idea for dogs, too. All Mrs Herbert had to do if her tortoise had disappeared was to say, 'Fetch Caroline,' and Busy would rush out and come trotting back with Caroline dangling from her mouth on the string handle. Caroline had her soppy expression and her head waving, not exactly furiously, but fast for a tortoise. It was a most affecting sight.

Earlier in this story I told you I'd explain the word 'hibernating', didn't I? Now's the time to do the explaining, because otherwise you might think it has a sad ending, which it hasn't.

All tortoises hibernate. They go to sleep early

in November and don't wake up again until the warm spring weather arrives. It's a jolly good idea in some ways to miss the winter, except that they miss Christmas as well. But that doesn't matter much to a tortoise, does it, because they don't eat turkey and wouldn't be able to pull crackers, anyway. Last winter Caroline started to hibernate as usual, and Busy was heart-broken because her tortoise friend wouldn't stick out her head and wag it any more. For a time Busy tried to hibernate as well. She put her head on Caroline's shell and closed her eyes and pretended to go to sleep. 'After all,' she said to herself, 'if a tortoise can hibernate, so can a poodle.' But she was wrong. Sleeping for an hour or two during the day and for most of the night is all very well, but hibernating for weeks and weeks is jolly boring, especially for a busy dog like Busy. So she gave it up and Caroline was put in the cellar in a box with leaves in the bottom to go on hibernating all by herself.

Somehow I don't think that Busy has forgotten her though. She's hoping that one day she'll be able to pick up her friend by the string handle and watch her wagging her head from side to side. Old Mrs Herbert and Bobby Brewster are anxiously waiting for that day too.

They needn't worry. When the warm spring weather comes Caroline *will* wake up, and she and Busy will play together happily again.